THE LITTLE GIRL WHO LOST HER WORDS

BY MJ ZONFRILLO

Illustrated by

SUE GRIGGS-BAILEY

Book design by Jeanne Balsam
jeannebalsamgraphics.com

© 2018 by MJ Zonfrillo
Visit MJ at mjzonfrillo.com
All rights reserved.

Library of Congress Control Number: 2018913998
Paperback ISBN: 978-0-9600367-0-7

Dedication

Dedicated to all the children who struggle to speak up ...
may they find their words!

Acknowledgments

Sue - I must start by thanking my awesome and talented illustrator, Sue Griggs-Bailey, for capturing the essence of Ava. You brought her story to life with beautiful illustrations. Thank you.

Jeanne - Jeanne Balsam, Graphic Designer/Editor, thank you for sharing your expertise and insightful feedback in readying this book for publication. Your patience and guidance were a gift to me. Thank you.

Loren/Just4Kids - The Just4Kids writing group and our mentor, Loren Spiotta-DiMare, have helped me through the many challenges of writing my first children's book. Your constant encouragement and guidance inspired me from our very first meeting. I couldn't have done it without you all. Thank you.

My Family - Much love and thanks to my husband and children for their encouragement and belief in me and this book. Also, to my grandchildren who show me something new every day, and especially my granddaughter, Ava, the inspiration of this book. Thank you.

Ava was so excited. Her Mom
brought her to school and
said that Grandpa was coming
to pick her up today.

"Is he bringing the big red
truck?" Ava asked.

Mom said, "Yes."

Ava daydreamed about sitting high up in Grandpa's truck and looking out the window.

It was three o'clock. Class was over, and the teacher told the children to put their jackets on and stand in line for dismissal.

THE DOORS OPENED AND THERE WAS
GRANDPA, WAITING WITH A BIG SMILE
ON HIS FACE.

Ava held Grandpa's hand and off they went.

Grandpa helped Ava into the truck and she buckled herself into her seat.

As they drove away, Grandpa asked, "How was school today, Ava?"

Ava opened her mouth to answer but no words came out.

Ava's eyes filled with tears. Grandpa was waiting for her answer.

Ava was so shy that she would put her words away so she didn't have to talk.

Now she couldn't remember where she put them.

She remembered using her words at school, but where did she put them?

Oh no, did she leave them at school?

GRANDPA ASKED AGAIN. WHEN AVA DID NOT
ANSWER, HE ASKED IF SHE FORGOT HER WORDS
AT SCHOOL.

AVA NODDED HER HEAD YES.

GRANDPA SAID, "WELL, LET'S GO BACK AND
FIND THEM!"

They drove back to school.

Ava jumped out of the red truck and
ran into her classroom.

Ava looked between the books, but there were no words!

WHERE COULD THEY BE?

Ava looked in her desk and found the pencil she'd lost!

But still no words.

She turned and looked in her cubby and she saw her green note.

It said, "it's always safe to use your words!"

She turned to Grandpa with
a smile on her face.

"Let's go home, Grandpa!"

IT'S ALWAYS SAFE
TO USE
YOUR WORDS.

Inspiration

THE INSPIRATION FOR THIS BOOK WAS A SHY BUT SMART LITTLE GIRL
NAMED AVA. SHE WOULD TUCK HER WORDS AWAY SO CAREFULLY THAT
SHE SOMETIMES DIDN'T KNOW WHERE TO FIND THEM WHEN SHE NEEDED THEM.

SOMETIMES WE WOULD SAY, "USE YOUR WORDS", BUT SHE JUST
COULDN'T ... AND SHE WOULD BECOME SO UPSET BECAUSE SHE
COULDN'T REMEMBER WHERE SHE PUT THEM.

SO MANY CHILDREN ARE UNCOMFORTABLE TO SPEAK UP IN SCHOOL.
THEY FIND IT DIFFICULT TO INTERACT WITH OTHERS. THIS BOOK IS FOR
ALL THE GIRLS AND BOYS WHO ARE AFRAID TO TALK ...

SPEAK UP! WE WOULD LOVE TO HEAR FROM YOU!

Thoughts about Ava's Lost Words

* WHY DO YOU THINK AVA FELT SHY?

* HOW DID SHE OVERCOME LOSING HER WORDS?

* WHO HELPED HER?

* DID YOU THINK AVA WOULD FIND HER WORDS?

* WHERE DID YOU THINK THEY WOULD BE?

* DO YOU EVER FEEL SHY?

* WHAT DO YOU DO WHEN YOU FEEL SHY?

Biography

MJ Zonfrillo

MJ IS A FIRST-TIME AUTHOR, MEMBER OF THE SOCIETY OF CHILDREN'S BOOK WRITERS & ILLUSTRATORS, AND A PROUD FOUNDING MEMBER OF JUST4KIDS, A LOCAL WRITERS' GROUP. MJ PREVIOUSLY WORKED IN THE EDUCATION FIELD FOR 27 YEARS, AND AFTER HER RECENT RETIREMENT, FOUND THE TIME TO WRITE THIS SPECIAL BOOK … THE FIRST OF A SERIES OF ADVENTURES WITH AVA.

MJ CURRENTLY LIVES IN NEW JERSEY WITH HER HUSBAND. SHE HAS FOUR CHILDREN, FIVE GRANDCHILDREN, AND A GRAND DOG. HER INTERESTS INCLUDE YOGA, MEDITATION, SEWING, AND READING. SHE VOLUNTEERS AS A BOARD MEMBER AT A LOCAL SENIOR CITIZEN HOUSING CENTER AND CROCHETS FOR VARIOUS CHILDREN'S HOSPITALS. HER LIFE HAS INCLUDED INTERNATIONAL TRAVEL, BECOMING A COFFEE AND TEA ENTREPRENEUR, AND A FENG SHUI PRACTITIONER WITH A UNIQUE MEDITATION GARDEN. MJ BRINGS HER GENTLE SPIRIT EVERYWHERE SHE GOES.

Sue Griggs-Bailey

NEW JERSEY BORN, AND A GRADUATE OF PAIER SCHOOL OF ART, SUE GRIGGS-BAILEY IS A PROFESSIONAL PASTEL AND MIXED MEDIA ARTIST.

SHE HAS EXHIBITED HER WORK IN NEW JERSEY AND EASTPORT, MAINE GALLERIES. THIS IS HER FIRST EXPERIENCE ILLUSTRATING A CHILDREN'S BOOK.

Made in the USA
Middletown, DE
01 March 2019